THE DRAGON STOORWORM

RETOLD BY
THERESA BRESLIN

ILLUSTRATED BY
MATTHEW LAND

The Dragon Stoorworm was the very first, and the very worst, dragon ever to exist from the beginning of time. It was absolutely gi***nor***mous and almost completely covered Scotland, from the top to the bottom, and all the way across from side to side.

Soon after the Dragon Stoorworm arrived in Scotland, it had eaten whole herds of sheep, drunk dry most of the lochs, and burned half the crops with long flickers of flame that shot out of its mouth. It promised to stop if it could have just one delicious young person to eat every day, starting with the king's daughter, the Princess Gemdelovely.

The king was very upset. He announced that he would give his sword, his kingdom and the hand of his daughter in marriage to anyone who could free Scotland from the Dragon Stoorworm.

Princess Gemdelovely said, "Papa, the sword and the kingdom are yours to give, but my hand belongs to me. I will choose the person I marry!"

Many warriors came to the king to enquire about his sword and his kingdom and, after that, about the Princess Gemdelovely. They went to do battle with the Dragon Stoorworm, but they never came back. Sometimes a stirrup or helmet was found, which the Dragon Stoorworm had spat out on the shores of the loch.

Although Princess Gemdelovely was sad for these warriors, none of them had touched her heart. Then, one day, a boy called Assipattle wandered along the road.

Assipattle was a bit different from the warriors who rushed around fighting. He liked to sing and sit by the fire making up stories.

He was walking and singing by the castle when Princess Gemdelovely looked from her window and thought, "Aha ..."

Assipattle glanced up and saw the Princess Gemdelovely. He thought, "Aha ..."

Assipattle went into the castle and said to the king, "I've seen a girl in your tower who has an honest, interesting look. I'd like to talk with her and share my stories."

Princess Gemdelovely stepped from behind a curtain where she'd been listening and said, "I'd like to meet you too."

Assipattle held out his hand and Princess Gemdelovely took it in her own.

"Hold on a minute," said the king. "First, Scotland has to be saved from the Dragon Stoorworm. Whoever does that may marry the Princess Gemdelovely."

"Well," said Assipattle, "the Princess Gemdelovely should marry whom she chooses. But," he turned to the princess, "would it be best to get rid of the Stoorworm before we chat about our favourite stories?"

"That would be very helpful," said Princess Gemdelovely.

Early next morning, Princess Gemdelovely and Assipattle crept into a tiny boat on the loch near where the Dragon Stoorworm was sleeping. When the Stoorworm awoke, it opened its great jaws, yawned mightily, and took in a huge drink.

The tiny boat was swept along as the loch water rushed into its vast mouth. Princess Gemdelovely and Assipattle rowed as fast as they were able, past the sharp teeth, over the dreadful tongue and down the throat of the monster.

They hung on as the boat was battered every which way until finally they reached the Stoorworm's stomach. Princess Gemdelovely held the boat steady as Assipattle took a knife and dug a hole in the flesh of the Stoorworm. Next Princess Gemdelovely opened a jar containing a glowing peat that they'd taken from the fire in the castle. They blew on the peat, not once, not twice, but three times, to make it blaze like a live coal. Then they rammed the peat deep into the hole in the stomach of the Stoorworm.

Very soon the fire from the peat began to hurt the Stoorworm. As it got hotter and hotter the Stoorworm started to roll and writhe. The more its stomach burned, the more it howled. It screeched and screamed, then tried to get rid of the burning in its belly by gagging and spewing.

And so, all the water and the tiny boat with Princess Gemdelovely and Assipattle in it flowed out of the Stoorworm's mouth and back into the loch.

As the little boat heaved about, Assipattle stood up. Princess Gemdelovely handed him the king's sword, and Assipattle skelped the Stoorworm the most tremendous blow on the side of its head. Assipattle struck with such force that the Stoorworm was sent rocketing into the sky.

Assipattle kissed Princess Gemdelovely three times and asked if she'd marry him. Princess Gemdelovely kissed Assipattle seven times and decided that she would. And so they lived long and happily together in the country of Scotland.

And what became of the Dragon Stoorworm?

Well, Assipattle gave its head such a clatter that its teeth flew out. They splashed down all around Scotland, forming islands and rocks.

The Stoorworm's body went north, landing with a terrific thud near the top of the world. The sea hissed and boiled for a while, but then the cold Arctic Ocean froze over the gigantic lump, and it is now the country called Iceland.

Every so often an enormous belch of smoke and fire bursts from the earth there. Some people say that this is a volcano erupting – but it is really the Dragon Stoorworm snoring in its sleep.